To: _____

From: _____

"May the Lord watch between you
and me when we are absent one
from the other."
— Genesis 31:49

Visit us on the Web!
rhcbooks.com
BerenstainBears.com

Educators and librarians, for a variety of teaching tools, visit us at RHTeachersLibrarians.com

ISBN 978-0-593-30244-6 (trade) — ISBN 978-0-593-30522-5 (ebook)

MANUFACTURED IN CHINA
10 9 8 7 6 5 4 3 2 1

The Berenstain Bears.
Gifts of the Spirit
Family

Mike Berenstain

Based on the characters created by
Stan and Jan Berenstain

Random House 🏠 **New York**

Everyone who saw the bright balloons tied to the mailbox in front of the Bear family's tree house assumed they were having a party. And, of course, they were right! Today was Brother Bear's birthday.

The tree house was decorated with balloons, streamers, and big HAPPY BIRTHDAY signs. The dining room table was prepared with party settings and party hats—everything was ready for the cutting of Brother's birthday cake.

In a happy daze, Brother watched the preparations going on around him. After all, he didn't have much to do—he *was* the birthday boy! The only trouble was . . . he was soon a bored birthday boy.

"Is there anything I can do?" he asked as Mama bustled past. "Not really, sweetie!" said Mama, giving him a hug. "We're almost ready for the rest of the family."

"Are Uncle Tex and Aunt May really coming?" asked Brother. They lived out West and didn't get East very often.

"Yes," said Mama. "They're in town visiting Gramps and Gran."

"Great!" said Brother. Uncle Tex and Aunt May were a lot of fun, and he was always glad to see them.

Mama gave Brother another hug, and a tear came to her eye.
"What's the matter, Mama?" asked Brother, alarmed.

"Nothing!" she replied. "I'm just so happy. It seems like only yesterday you were a fat little baby, and now look at you!"

"Aw, Mama!" said Brother, blushing.

Sister and Honey overheard them. "A fat little baby?" they said. "Do tell!"

"Well, all you cubs were chubby," said Mama. Sister and Honey were shocked. "After all," Mama said, "we're bears! You don't often see a skinny bear."

Mama took their family album down from the shelf and opened it.

"See?" she said, pointing out some baby photos of the cubs. "Weren't you all adorable?"

The cubs had to admit they were awfully cute!
Mama couldn't resist gathering them all up for
another big Mama Bear hug.

"You three are such a blessing to your papa and me!" she said, squeezing them tight.

"Really?" wheezed Brother, gasping for breath. He had never thought of himself as a blessing. "Are we a blessing even when we're bad?"

Papa, who was on a stepladder stringing up a birthday sign, chimed in.

"Oh, you're never *that* bad, Son!" he said, laughing. "Besides, we're all a family, and families are always a blessing!"

The cubs thought it over. Maybe Papa had a point. They remembered all the things their family had done together—all the joking and laughing, all the crying and yelling, all the playing and picnicking, all the accidents and adventures, the happy times, the tough times, the triumphs and defeats. It was all part of being a family.

"Mama," said Sister thoughtfully, "what are your favorite family times?"

"For me," said Mama, "the most precious are the plain, ordinary, everyday ones, like reading stories at bedtime, or going for a walk on a crisp autumn day, or gathering around a cozy fire on a snowy evening—just being together!"

The cubs remembered one snowy Christmas Eve a few years back. The whole family had gone sledding in the twilight. As they trudged home through the darkening woods, tired but happy, they could see the Christmas lights on their tree house. Their home looked so warm and welcoming as it twinkled through the trees. That was a very special moment for the family.

Then the doorbell rang, and their dream of the past vanished. Cousin Fred, Uncle Ned, Aunt Min, and baby Teddi had arrived.

And right behind them were Gramps and Gran with Uncle Tex and Aunt May, all bearing lots of birthday presents!

"Thanks for invitin' us to your birthday shindig!" said Aunt May, giving Brother an especially powerful bear hug.

"Happy birthday there, Brother!" said Uncle Tex, shaking hands. He leaned down to whisper, "Hope you like your presents!" Brother nodded in excitement. The last time they'd met, he mentioned he'd always wanted a cowboy hat and boots.

Soon, it was time to sit down for cake and ice cream. The family put on some party hats and tooted party horns.

"Happy birthday, dear Brother! Happy birthday to you!" they all sang.

To Brother, it seemed like the best birthday party ever. Why? Because so much of his family was there—and, as far as he was concerned, the more family, the better!

He took a deep breath and blew out all the candles on his cake in one mighty puff!

"Way to go, Brother!" everyone cried as they settled down to eat some yummy birthday cake.